The Polka Dot Ice Cream Club

Written and Illustrated

by

Zwanjay Brown

ISBN:

ISBN-13: 9781092257237

To my daughters – Thank you for keeping me young.

The Polka Dot Ice Cream Club

By Zwanjay Brown

Every Saturday, Petey and his mom went to the town center to shop. Petey liked going shopping with his mom. He looked in every store window to see what was for sale.

One day, Petey saw something wonderful in the window of Major's Toy Store -- it was a shiny toy airplane!

The toy airplane was silver and red with lots of windows all around. Petey thought the airplane would be fun to play with.

"Mom, can we buy the big airplane?" Petey asked.
"It's only five dollars."

Petey's mom didn't even look at the airplane.

"You have enough toys already." she said.

"if you want that airplane, you'll have to buy it
yourself."

When Petey got home, he shook all of the money out of his piggy bank . . .

and then he looked for coins under the couch . . .
and then he charged his dad two dollars to rake the leaves . . .

But he still didn't have enough money for the airplane Petey was very, very sad.

"Cheer up," said Petey's dad. "You may not have enough money for the airplane, but you have enough for ice cream."

"Ice cream?" asked Petey. "What does ice cream have to do with anything?"

"You can buy ice cream and sell it," explained Petey's dad. "That way you can earn the money you need to buy the airplane."

Petey thought that was a great idea. He couldn't wait to start.

Petey's mom took him to the grocery store to buy the ice cream, and his dad helped him build an ice cream stand next to the refrigerator in the garage.

In a few hours, Petey was open for business!

Petey sold ice cream to the man next door and his friend across the street, but nobody else came to buy ice cream from him.

Petey asked his mom, "What's wrong with my ice cream? Nobody wants it."

"Maybe it's too plain." said Petey's mom. "You have to think of something fun that will make people want to try your ice cream."

Petey was sad again. He didn't know how to make people want to try his ice cream.

Just then, Petey's friend Tom came over
eating his favorite treat: a bag of colorful
round pieces of candy called Polka Dots.
   "What's up, Petey?" said Tom.
   "I'm trying to sell ice cream," said Petey.
"But nobody wants it because it is too plain."

"We just have to brain storm," said Tom. "If we both think really hard, I'm sure we can come up with some great ice cream flavors that everyone will love."

"Oh yeah?" Petey frowned. "Like what?"

"You could make banana splits." suggested Tom.

"I don't have any bananas." Petey answered.

"What about fresh strawberries? That's what my mom always does." said Tom.

Petey moaned, "I don't have any strawberries either. I might as well give up; I'll never get enough money for my toy airplane."

"Don't give up yet," encouraged Tom. "Let's go inside and see what you have."

As the boys headed inside, Tom slipped on one of Petey's skates

and his colorful round candy went flying everywhere . . .

But mostly in the ice cream!

When everyone on Petey'sstreet saw the colorful ice cream, they all wanted to try some. People started buying double and triple scoops of Petey and Tom's polka dot ice cream until it was all gone. Petey made more than enough money to buy the shiny toy airplane.

Petey's mom took him to buy the shiny airplane, but he didn't want it anymore. He wanted to buy more ice cream instead.

Petey asked his dad to help him build a clubhouse so that he could start a special group called the polka dot ice cream club -- a club just for ice cream lovers!

The polka dot ice cream club would sit in their clubhouse and make up all kinds of ice cream flavors for people to enjoy. Petey thought it would be so much fun that everyone would soon want to join.

And Petey was right! Every kid in the neighborhood came over to join Petey and Tom's polka dot ice cream club. They had enough members to fill their clubhouse.

. . . And everybody's favorite thing was trying the new ice cream flavors, like candy bar crunch, straw-cano, pink pineapple, and blueberry waves. Yummy!

The End

Made in the USA
Middletown, DE
21 May 2019